Michael Morpurgo studied philosophy and modern languages before becoming a teacher. He now runs Farms for City Children, an educational charity, with his wife. He has written more than 60 books, including *Why the Whales Came*, which was made into a full-length feature film starring Helen Mirren and Paul Schofield. Other titles include *Wreck of the Zanzibar* (1995, HarperCollins) which won the Whitbread Award in 1995 and was nominated for the IBBY Honour Book of 1998, *Butterfly Lion* (1996, Egmont) which won the 1996 Smarties Gold Award and the Children's Book Prize and most recently *Kensuke's Kingdom* (1999, Mammoth) which won the Children's Book Award 2000.

Christina Balit studied at Chelsea School of Art and the Royal College of Art. In 1982 she won a Thames Television Travelling Design Bursary and illustrated *Report to Greco* by Niko Kazantisakis. Christina has had an incredibly successful relationship with Frances Lincoln. Her first book was *Blodin the Beast* which was shortlisted for the 1995 Kate Greenaway Medal; her next, *Ishtar and Tammuz* by Christopher Moore was commended for the 1996 Kate Greenaway Medal and *The Twelve Labours of Hercules* by James Riordan received a nomination for the Kate Greenaway Medal in 1997. She also illustrated *Zoo in the Sky* by Jacqueline Mitton which received one of the English Association 4-11 Awards for the Best Children's Picture Book of 1998 and W*omen of Camelot* written by Mary Hoffman, which was published in September 2000. *Atlantis*, the first book she both illustrated and wrote for Frances Lincoln, was published in 1999 to great acclaim.

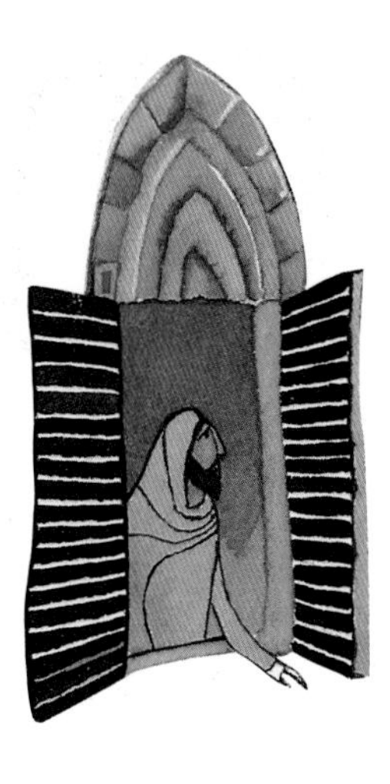

• *For Graham, Isabella, Alex, Robbie and Mairi - M.M*

• *For Sean-George - C.B.*

•

First published in Great Britain in 1995 by
Frances Lincoln Limited, 4 Torriano Mews, Torriano Avenue, London NW5 2RZ

First paperback edition 1996

British Library Cataloguing in Publication Data available on request

ISBN 0-7112-0910-3 paperback

Set in Garamond Book

Printed in Hong Kong

5 7 9 8 6 4

BLODIN THE BEAST

MICHAEL
MORPURGO

•

Illustrated by
CHRISTINA
BALIT

FRANCES LINCOLN

Blodin the beast stalked the land. He drank only oil, he breathed only fire. When he roared, the earth shook and the people trembled. Town after town he razed to ruins, village after village.

No sword, no spear could pierce his thick, horny hide. No one could stand against him. Some tried, but were scorched at once to ashes.

There was no hiding place. There was nowhere to run, except to the mountains, and everyone knew the mountains went on for ever. Up there you would die of hunger or cold or both. Better to become Blodin's slave. Better to dig his oil for him than to die.

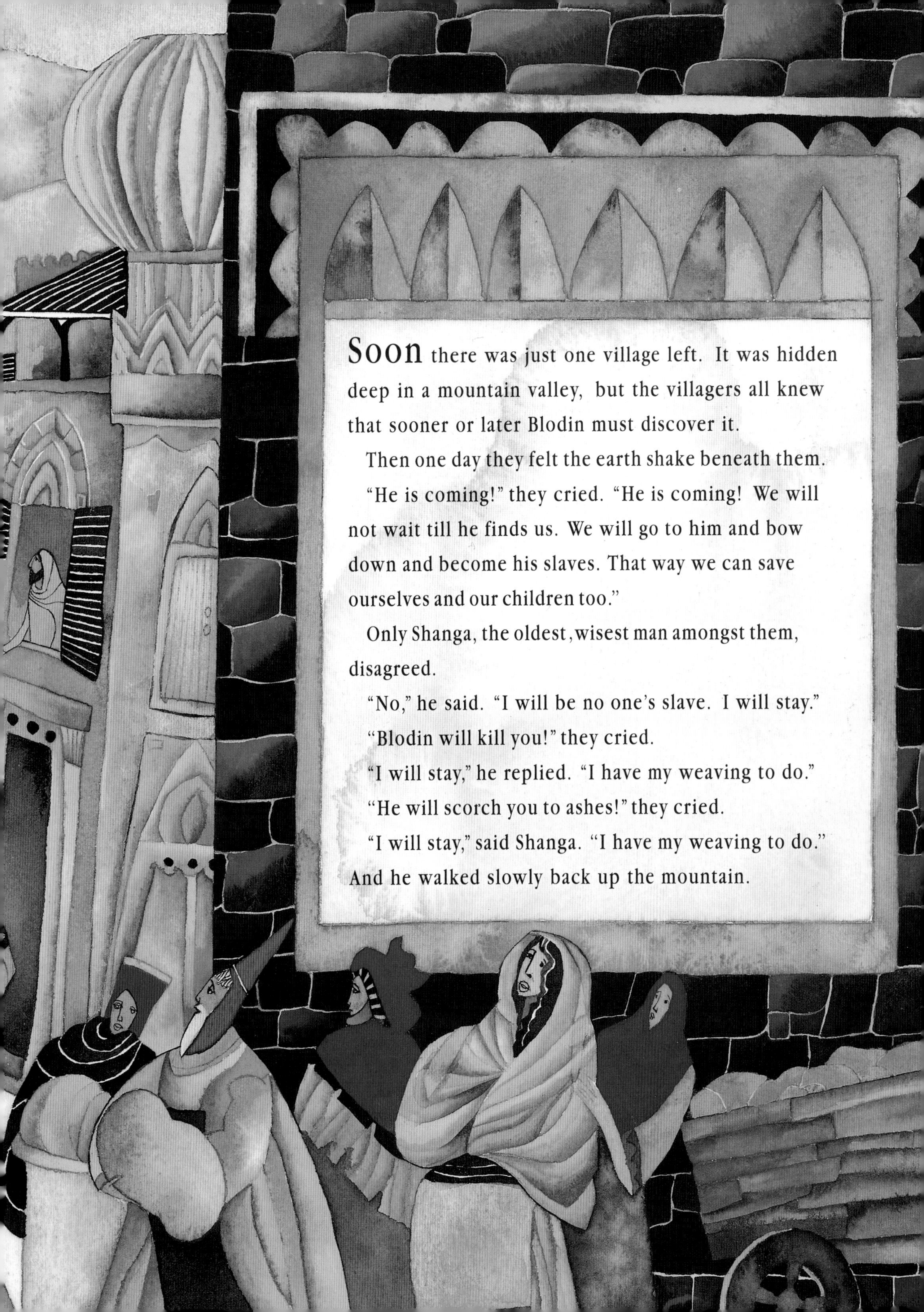

Soon there was just one village left. It was hidden deep in a mountain valley, but the villagers all knew that sooner or later Blodin must discover it.

Then one day they felt the earth shake beneath them.

"He is coming!" they cried. "He is coming! We will not wait till he finds us. We will go to him and bow down and become his slaves. That way we can save ourselves and our children too."

Only Shanga, the oldest, wisest man amongst them, disagreed.

"No," he said. "I will be no one's slave. I will stay."

"Blodin will kill you!" they cried.

"I will stay," he replied. "I have my weaving to do."

"He will scorch you to ashes!" they cried.

"I will stay," said Shanga. "I have my weaving to do." And he walked slowly back up the mountain.

Old Shanga lived in a cave above the village. For as long as anyone could remember, he had sat cross-legged in the mouth of the cave weaving his carpet. It was only a small carpet, yet he never seemed to finish it.

Now, one by one, the villagers came to say their goodbyes. Last of all came Hosea, a young boy with no family of his own. He looked at old Shanga, whom he loved like a father.

"I will not leave you here to die alone," he said. "Let me stay with you."

"Very well, my son," said Shanga with tears in his eyes, "but when Blodin comes, and he is not far away now, you must promise to do as I say."

Hosea promised.

"And now I must finish my carpet," said old Shanga.

"But you never finish it," Hosea said.

"When you finish your life's work, you die," said old Shanga. "My life's work is to destroy Blodin the beast. You will see, my son, that there is more than wool in this carpet."

That night, as Hosea slept, Shanga finished his carpet.

The next morning it seemed as if the sun did not rise as it should. The earth shook, and Blodin the beast came stalking over the mountains, smothering the sun with his thick black smoke. Hosea and old Shanga watched from the cave as he breathed his fire on the village and burnt it to the ground.

Behind him came his slaves, thousands of them, the villagers amongst them. He set them digging for oil all over the valley, and then sat down on the hillside to watch over them. But as he watched he fell asleep.

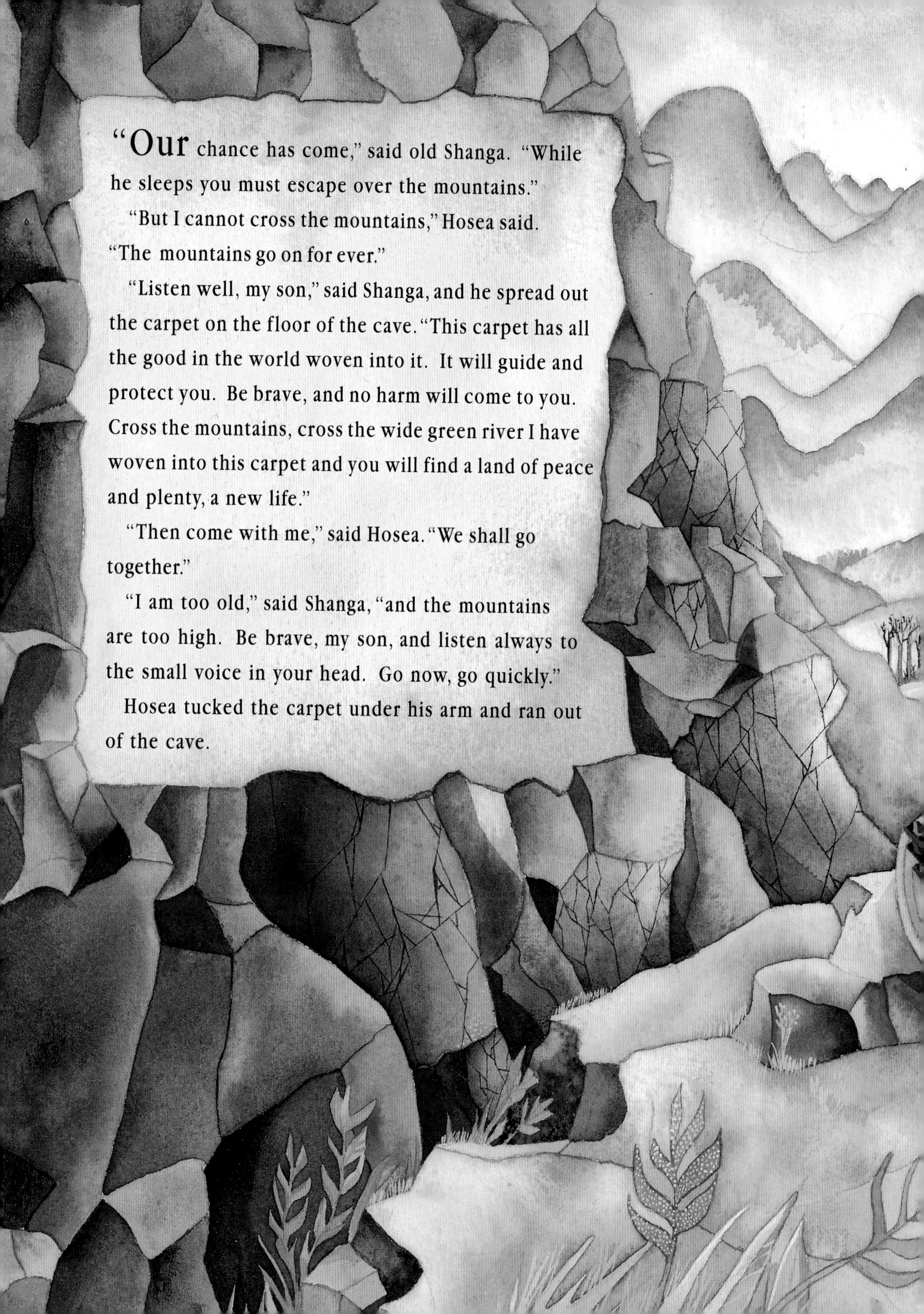

"Our chance has come," said old Shanga. "While he sleeps you must escape over the mountains."

"But I cannot cross the mountains," Hosea said. "The mountains go on for ever."

"Listen well, my son," said Shanga, and he spread out the carpet on the floor of the cave. "This carpet has all the good in the world woven into it. It will guide and protect you. Be brave, and no harm will come to you. Cross the mountains, cross the wide green river I have woven into this carpet and you will find a land of peace and plenty, a new life."

"Then come with me," said Hosea. "We shall go together."

"I am too old," said Shanga, "and the mountains are too high. Be brave, my son, and listen always to the small voice in your head. Go now, go quickly."

Hosea tucked the carpet under his arm and ran out of the cave.

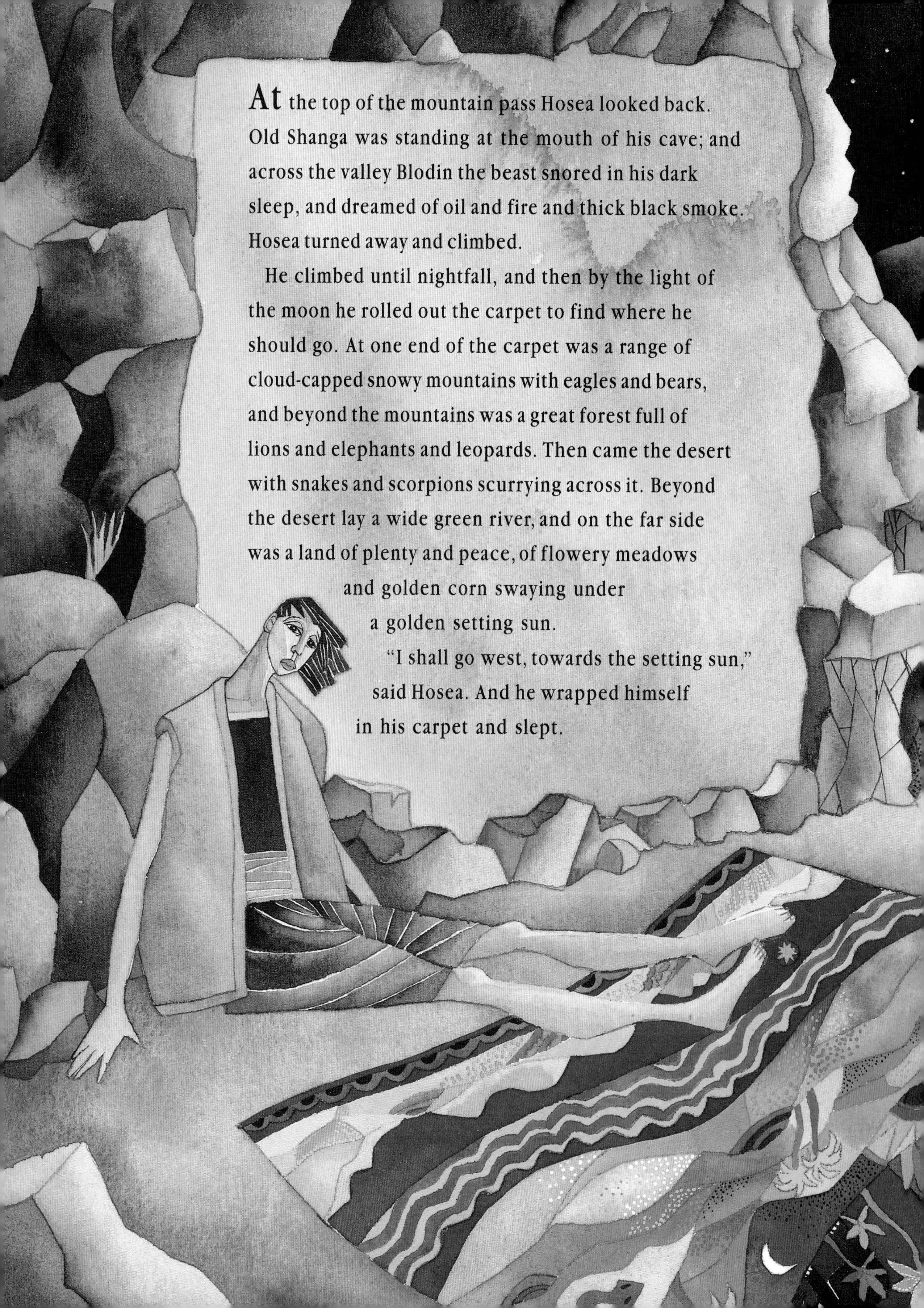

At the top of the mountain pass Hosea looked back. Old Shanga was standing at the mouth of his cave; and across the valley Blodin the beast snored in his dark sleep, and dreamed of oil and fire and thick black smoke. Hosea turned away and climbed.

He climbed until nightfall, and then by the light of the moon he rolled out the carpet to find where he should go. At one end of the carpet was a range of cloud-capped snowy mountains with eagles and bears, and beyond the mountains was a great forest full of lions and elephants and leopards. Then came the desert with snakes and scorpions scurrying across it. Beyond the desert lay a wide green river, and on the far side was a land of plenty and peace, of flowery meadows and golden corn swaying under a golden setting sun.

"I shall go west, towards the setting sun," said Hosea. And he wrapped himself in his carpet and slept.

The next day the sun rose as it should.

"Blodin the beast must still be asleep," said Hosea.

He rolled up his carpet and made his way over the mountains and down into the forests below - always westward. He swallowed the fear rising in his throat as eagles soared above him, bears lumbered after him, lions padded towards him, elephants trumpeted at him and leopards loped along behind him like spotted shadows.

"Be brave," said the small voice in his head. And he was, and none of them came near him.

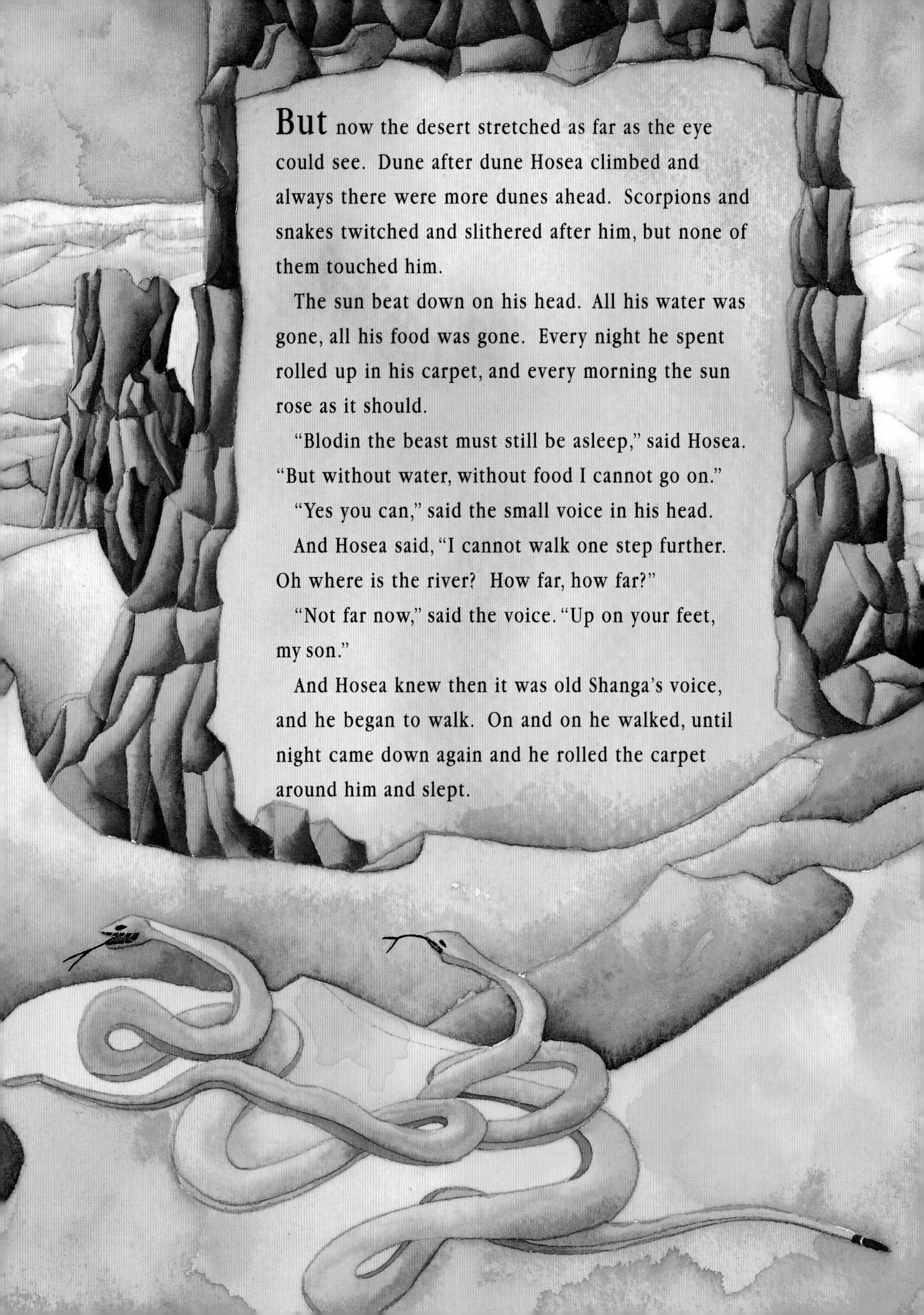

But now the desert stretched as far as the eye could see. Dune after dune Hosea climbed and always there were more dunes ahead. Scorpions and snakes twitched and slithered after him, but none of them touched him.

The sun beat down on his head. All his water was gone, all his food was gone. Every night he spent rolled up in his carpet, and every morning the sun rose as it should.

"Blodin the beast must still be asleep," said Hosea. "But without water, without food I cannot go on."

"Yes you can," said the small voice in his head.

And Hosea said, "I cannot walk one step further. Oh where is the river? How far, how far?"

"Not far now," said the voice. "Up on your feet, my son."

And Hosea knew then it was old Shanga's voice, and he began to walk. On and on he walked, until night came down again and he rolled the carpet around him and slept.

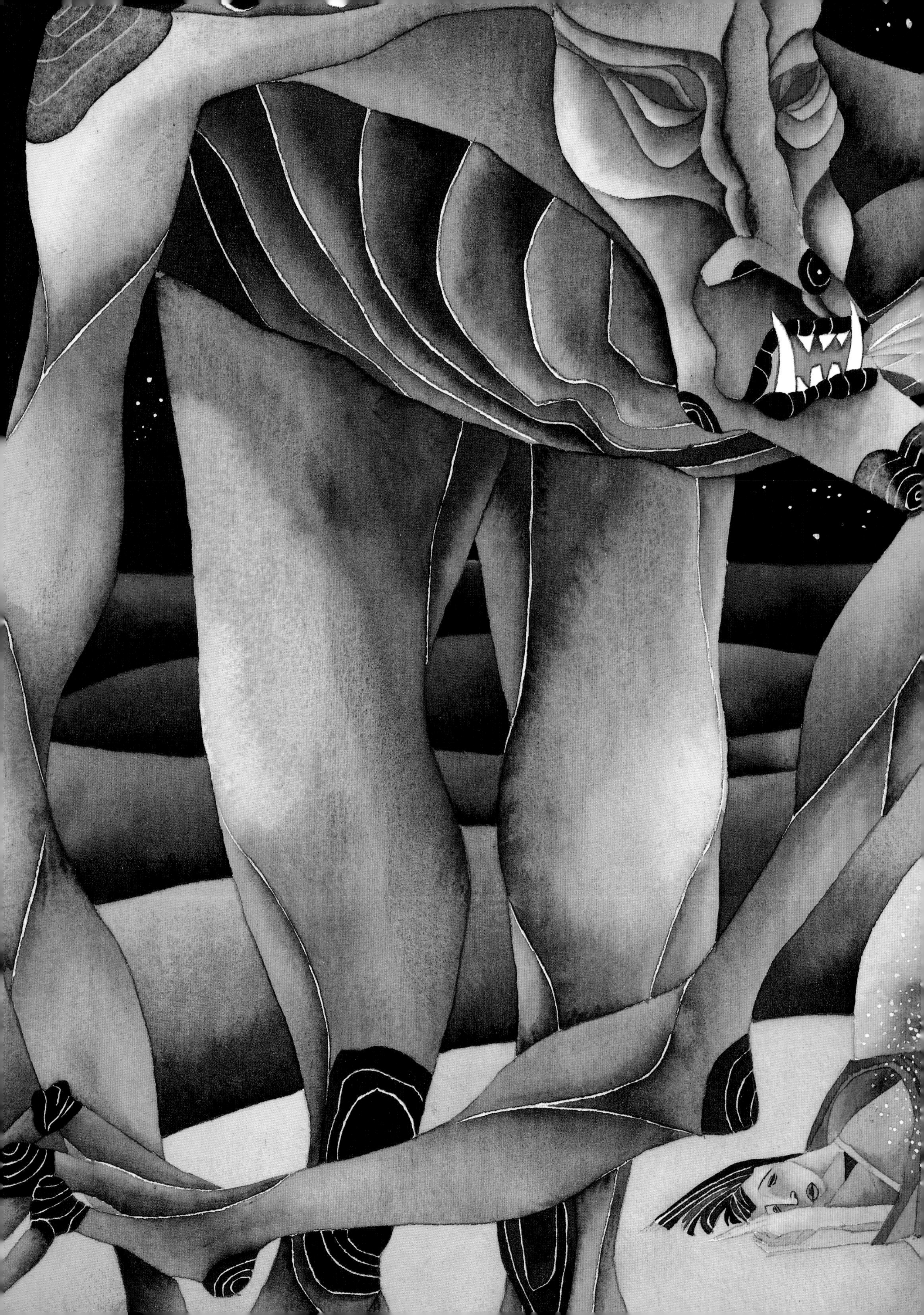

And as he slept, he dreamed a dream.

Old Shanga stood leaning on a stick outside his cave with Blodin the beast towering above him.

"I will be no one's slave," old Shanga told him. "You may think yourself the strongest, but you are not. You may think you have conquered the world, but you have not. Up in the mountains is a small boy and he is stronger than you. He carries with him only a small carpet, but with it he will destroy you."

Blodin roared, and the smoke from his fire covered Shanga, and Hosea saw him no more.

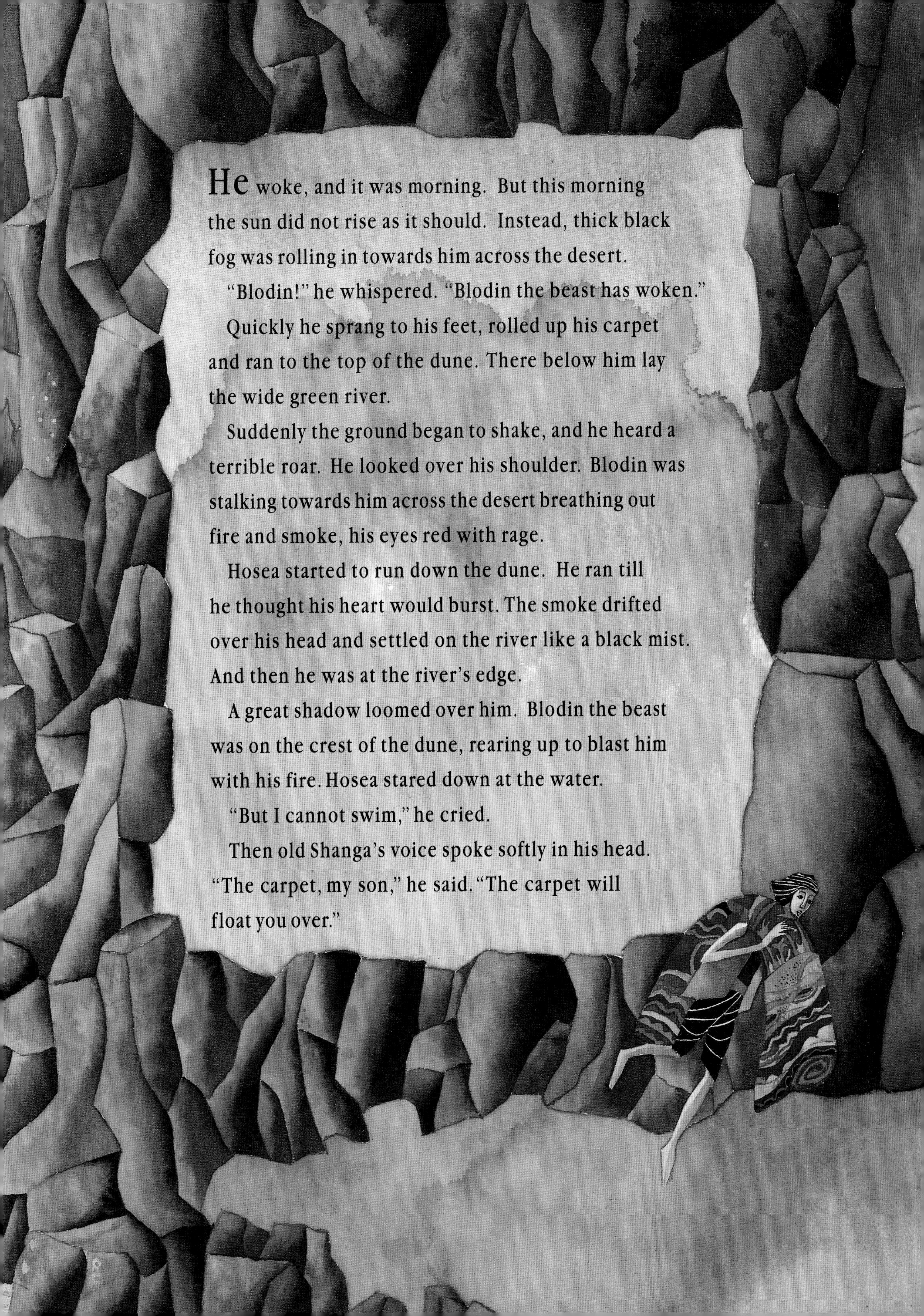

He woke, and it was morning. But this morning the sun did not rise as it should. Instead, thick black fog was rolling in towards him across the desert.

"Blodin!" he whispered. "Blodin the beast has woken."

Quickly he sprang to his feet, rolled up his carpet and ran to the top of the dune. There below him lay the wide green river.

Suddenly the ground began to shake, and he heard a terrible roar. He looked over his shoulder. Blodin was stalking towards him across the desert breathing out fire and smoke, his eyes red with rage.

Hosea started to run down the dune. He ran till he thought his heart would burst. The smoke drifted over his head and settled on the river like a black mist. And then he was at the river's edge.

A great shadow loomed over him. Blodin the beast was on the crest of the dune, rearing up to blast him with his fire. Hosea stared down at the water.

"But I cannot swim," he cried.

Then old Shanga's voice spoke softly in his head. "The carpet, my son," he said. "The carpet will float you over."

So Hosea spread the carpet on the water and threw himself on to it. As he floated out across the river through the choking black smoke, he could hear Blodin snarling and splashing after him. He dared not look. He dared not hope.

Angry flames licked around him now, but he felt no heat, though everywhere the water boiled and bubbled. He feared the carpet might sink, but it did not. He feared he would be scorched to ashes, but he was not. Then he felt the shore beneath the carpet, and he leapt off.

He heard behind him a terrible shriek, and a blast of steam hurled him to the ground. When he turned to look, the last of Blodin was sinking beneath the hissing waters of the river.

"Blodin the beast is destroyed," said old Shanga's voice in his head. "All that was needed was an old man's faith and a young man's courage. My life's work is done, my son, but yours is just beginning. God go with you."

As Hosea got to his feet, the smoke drifted away and he could see flowery meadows and golden corn swaying under a golden sun.

There were men and women working together in the fields, and laughing children ran towards him. They took him by the hand and led him up into a land of plenty and peace.

OTHER PICTURE BOOKS IN PAPERBACK FROM FRANCES LINCOLN

ISHTAR AND TAMMUZ

Christopher Moore

Illustrated by Christina Balit

Ishtar, all-powerful queen of the stars, sends her son Tammuz down to the Earth she has created. Life flourishes wherever he walks, and Ishtar, growing jealous of how much he is loved, banishes him to the underworld. In his absence, the Earth slowly begins to die.

Commended for the 1997 Kate Greenaway Medal

Suitable for National Curriculum English — Reading, Key Stage 2; History, Key Stage 2
Scottish Guidelines English Language — Reading, Levels C and D; Environmental Studies, Levels C and D

ISBN 0-7112-1099-3

ZOO IN THE SKY

Jacqueline Mitton

Illustrated by Christina Balit

Distinguished astronomer and writer Dr Jacqueline Mitton takes us on a magical tour of the skies, featuring 19 constellations named after animals, birds and fishes. The poetic text combines with Christina Balit's incandescent paintings to create a book which will fascinate children of all ages.

Suitable for National Curriculum English — Reading, Key Stages 1 and 2; Science, Key Stages 1 and 2
Scottish Guidelines English Language — Reading, Levels C and D; Environmental Studies, Levels B, C and D

ISBN 0-7112-1319-4

THE TWELVE LABOURS OF HERCULES

James Riordan

Illustrated by Christina Balit

Everyone has heard of Hercules — but few can name the feats of strength which made him the greatest of mortal men and mythology's mightiest hero. Now, James Riordan's bold retellings of the ancient Greek legends re-create the labours of Zeus' much-loved son. A heroic anthology that children will reach for again and again.

Suitable for National Curriculum English — Reading, Key Stages 2 and 3; History, Key Stage 2
Scottish Guidelines English Language — Reading, Levels D and E; Environmental Studies — Levels C, D and E.

ISBN 0-7112-1391-7